Airy Fairy

Magic Mess!

This book belongs to:

Tahiya

Look out for more stories...

Magic Mischief!

Magic Muddle!

Airy Fairy

Magic Mess!

Margaret Ryan
illustrated by Teresa Murfin

■ SCHOLASTIC

To Matilda, with love

Scholastic Children's Books,
Commonwealth House, 1-19 New Oxford Street,
London, WC1A 1NU, UK
a division of Scholastic Ltd
London ~ New York ~ Toronto ~ Sydney ~ Auckland
Mexico City ~ New Delhi ~ Hong Kong

First published by Scholastic Ltd, 2004

Text copyright © Margaret Ryan, 2004
Illustrations copyright © Teresa Murfin, 2004

ISBN 0 439 96332 X
Fairs edition ISBN 0 439 95933 0

Printed and bound by Nørhaven Paperback A/S, Denmark

2 4 6 8 10 9 7 5 3 1

Chapter One

Spring had arrived at Fairy Gropplethorpe's Academy for Good Fairies, and Miss Stickler and the fairies were decorating the school hall with the bowls of spring flowers they had grown.

"Look how pretty my snowdrops are," said Buttercup.

"Look how bright my yellow crocuses are," said Tingle.

"I don't know what's happened to mine," said Airy Fairy. "I've only got green shoots."

"You never get anything right, Airy Fairy," smirked Scary Fairy. "I bet you planted the wrong bulbs. Anyway, my bowl is easily the best. Fairy Gropplethorpe's bound to say so."

Airy Fairy sighed and took her seat for assembly. It was always the same. Scary Fairy got everything right, while she always seemed to get everything wrong. No matter how hard she tried.

When Fairy Gropplethorpe came into the hall, the ten little fairies stood up politely, but Fairy Gropplethorpe waved them back to their seats.

"Good morning, Fairies," she smiled. "It's a beautiful morning, and made all the more lovely by your spring flowers." And she stopped to admire them.

"What lovely snowdrops, Buttercup. What elegant narcissi, Cherri. And the crocuses so many of you planted are splendid, though surprisingly Scary Fairy's seem to have doubled in number," and she gave Scary Fairy a puzzled look. "I wonder how that happened?"

"Scary Fairy has green fingers," smiled Miss Stickler. Scary Fairy was her niece and Miss Stickler thought she was wonderful.

"But what's happened to this little bowl here?" said Fairy Gropplethorpe. "It has no flowers at all."

"That's Airy Fairy's bowl," sighed Miss Stickler. "I'm afraid she doesn't have green fingers."

Airy Fairy examined her fingers. She didn't know if she wanted them to be green, though perhaps multicoloured shiny stars on them would be nice if she was going to a party.

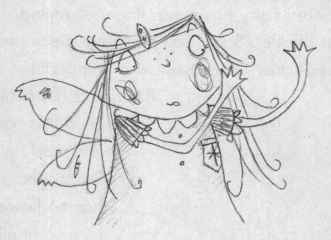

Fairy Gropplethorpe looked closely at Airy Fairy's bowl. "Actually Airy Fairy's bowl has done very well, it's just that she's planted spring onions instead of flowers."

The other fairies giggled. Airy Fairy always did funny things.

"Onions!" squeaked Airy Fairy. "I didn't mean to plant onions. How did that happen?" Then she remembered. Scary Fairy had handed her the bulbs to plant. This was another of her rotten tricks. She was always trying to get Airy Fairy into trouble.

"Sorry, Fairy Gropplethorpe," said Airy Fairy. "I didn't know… I mean, I didn't mean… I mean, sorry, Fairy Gropplethorpe."

But Fairy Gropplethorpe was smiling. "No need to apologize, Airy Fairy. Spring onions are very tasty, and when they're ready we can put them into a special pie and have it for tea. Well done."

Airy Fairy turned and made a cheeky face at Scary Fairy. Scary Fairy scowled.

Airy Fairy really loved the springtime. She loved the way the green shoots pushed their way out of the brown earth, and she loved to watch the baby animals and birds playing in the garden.

Fairy Gropplethorpe loved the springtime too. "But there is always so much to do after the long winter," she said, "and everything outside looking so fresh and new has given me an idea. I've been looking at some of your bedrooms..."

Oh help, thought Airy Fairy. *I hope she didn't look at mine. It's a bit messy.*

But Fairy Gropplethorpe wasn't worried about tidiness. "They all look a bit uninteresting painted plain white," she said. "So, after you've finished your work in class, you can have three magic spells to paint your bedrooms any colour you wish. I have to go away to a head teachers' conference for a few days, but when I come back Miss Stickler and I will choose the best bedroom and give this little prize to the successful fairy." And she held up the prettiest, daintiest fairy pen.

"Ooh," said the Fairies.

"Perhaps if I wrote with that I could get my school work right sometimes," said Airy Fairy.

"You've got no chance," muttered Scary Fairy, poking Airy Fairy with her wand. "I'm the cleverest fairy. I'll win that pen. Just wait and see."

"But before we think about painting or prizes, the bedrooms will have to be spring cleaned," warned Miss Stickler, who did worry about tidiness. "Some of them are very messy." And she frowned at Airy Fairy. "Very messy indeed. But you can all have three magic spells to do the cleaning."

"I'm off to my conference now," said Fairy Gropplethorpe. "Unfortunately dogs are not allowed, so please remember to look after Macduff while I'm gone. And happy painting, Fairies! I shall look forward to seeing your bright bedrooms when I return." Then away she flew.

The fairies all went back to their classroom, chatting about the news.

"I'm going to paint my room brilliant yellow," said Buttercup.

"I'm going to paint my room awesome orange," said Tingle.

"I don't know what colour to paint mine," said Airy Fairy. "I like the colour of the sea, but sometimes it's blue, sometimes it's green and sometimes it's turquoise."

"It won't matter what you do," smirked
Scary Fairy. "It won't be half as good as
mine. Mine is bound to be the best because
I'm the best at painting and spelling. And
you're the worst," she said to Airy Fairy, and
poked her with her wand again.

"Oh, go and jump in a slimy swamp," said
Airy Fairy, who poked her right back and
was immediately caught by Miss Stickler.

"You know poking with wands is against
the school rules, Airy Fairy. Lose one
magic cleaning-up spell."

Airy Fairy sighed. It was always the same. She was always the one who got caught, while Scary Fairy got away with everything.

"Never mind, Airy Fairy," whispered Buttercup and Tingle. "You can easily tidy up with two spells."

Airy Fairy sat down at her desk, cupped her chin in her hands, and gazed out of the classroom window. The bright spring sun was shining on Fairy Gropplethorpe's Academy, making its windows sparkle.

To passers-by, the school just looked like an abandoned tree house, high up in an old oak, but inside it was home to ten little orphaned fairies. Airy Fairy turned her gaze to the branches of the oak tree. The oak buds were getting fat and seemed about to burst at any moment.

"I wonder why the buds never burst while I'm looking at them?" she whispered to Buttercup and Tingle. "Do you think if I gaze at them long enough, I might see them pop?" And she screwed up her eyes and gazed at them really, really hard.

"Airy Fairy, what ARE you doing?" said Miss Stickler. "Stop making silly faces at the window and get on with your work."

"Yes, Miss Stickler. Sorry, Miss Stickler. But I wasn't making silly faces, I was just trying to see the oak buds growing. Do you think they just grow when I'm not looking. Do you think if I looked away, then back again really quickly, I could catch them growing? Or do you think they just grow at night time while everyone's asleep?"

"I think you should be paying attention to your lessons instead of gazing out of the window, Airy Fairy. No wonder you're at the bottom of the class."

Behind her, Scary Fairy chanted softly, "Stupid. Stupid."

Airy Fairy sighed and picked up her pencil. She looked at the difficult sums Miss Stickler had put on the blackboard:

If it takes three fairies three days to walk three kilometres, how many days will it take them to walk nine kilometres?

Oh dear, thought Airy Fairy, sticking her pencil in her mouth and giving the end a

good chew. *It's bound to take a long time.
Nine kilometres is a very long way for little
fairies to walk. They'll probably get blisters
and not be able to walk very fast. I got a
blister once and Fairy Gropplethorpe had to
put a sticking plaster on my heel. And where
will the fairies sleep, or will they walk all
through the night as well? If they do that
they'll get very tired. And hungry. I wonder if
they'll stop to have something to eat, or will
they take sandwiches
with them? Oh,
I don't know,
it's all far too
difficult.*

Then she had a brainwave. *Aha!* she
thought. *I bet this is a trick question. Miss
Stickler loves trick questions. We all know
fairies don't have to walk at all.*

And she smiled and wrote down in her fairy notebook:

Answer to question one:

It would take the fairies no time at all to walk nine kilometres because they could either fly or magic themselves there immediately.

She sat back, feeling pleased with herself. She was sure that was the right answer to question one.

But it wasn't.

"Airy Fairy," sighed Miss Stickler, when she looked at Airy Fairy's notebook. "In the spring, when everything has a new beginning, I had hoped that you might begin to be more sensible too, but obviously not.

Lose one more magic cleaning-up spell for writing silly answers, and stay behind at break-time to do more sums."

"Oh," Airy Fairy's eyes opened wide in surprise. "I didn't mean it to be a silly answer, Miss Stickler. I was just so sorry for those poor little fairies having to walk all that way…"

"It IS a long way for fairies to walk," nodded Cherri.

"My fairy shoes would be worn right through," agreed Honeysuckle.

But Miss Stickler wasn't listening. Airy Fairy gave a huge sigh. She was sure that answer had been right, and at break-time she and Buttercup and Tingle had planned to play with the red squirrel.

"Never mind, Airy Fairy," whispered Buttercup. "We can see him again soon."

"And the answer to the first sum is nine days," whispered Tingle.

"You'll be nine YEARS trying to work out the answers to the rest," sneered Scary Fairy. "I always said you were an idiot. You'll never get anything right."

"Yes, I will," muttered Airy Fairy, then looked at the long row of sums she had to do. "Just maybe not today."

Chapter Two

But Airy Fairy was determined to get things
right, so she concentrated really, really
hard, finished all her sums, and managed
to stay out of trouble all afternoon. PHEW!
Then, when Miss Stickler called a special
meeting after school, she put on her most
intelligent expression – both eyes wide
open and her tongue sticking out – and
listened very carefully.

"I have called this special meeting for two reasons," said Miss Stickler. "Reason one is to remind you what you must do to make your bedrooms clean and tidy."

"I know what we must do, Aunt Stickler," volunteered Scary Fairy. "All the windows must be cleaned, the room swept and dusted, and all the rubbish thrown out. I've done it already. My bedroom is spotless."

"Well done, Scary Fairy," beamed Miss Stickler. "I knew I could count on you."

Then she looked over at Airy Fairy.

Airy Fairy was finding her intelligent expression hard to keep up, so she had tucked in her tongue and was propping open her eyelids with her fingers.

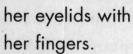

"Are you listening, Airy Fairy?"

"Oh yes," Airy Fairy nodded, and stuck a finger in her eye. That made her eye water and her nose run.

"Then repeat what it is you have to do."

"Er…" Airy Fairy blinked and sniffed. "Clean all the rubbish and throw it out of the window."

"Great idea, Airy Fairy," giggled twin fairies Twink and Plink.

"Look out, it's raining rubbish," giggled Skelf.

All the other fairies giggled too, except Scary Fairy who just muttered, "Idiot."

Miss Stickler frowned. "Just make sure your room is spotless, Airy Fairy. Remember you only have one cleaning-up spell left."

Airy Fairy gave up trying to look intelligent and blew out her cheeks instead. She hated tidying up. She could never find anything afterwards.

"Now," went on Miss Stickler, "the other reason for calling this special meeting is to let you into a secret. It's Fairy Gropplethorpe's Rainbow Birthday in three days' time, and I want you all to magic up a present for her. Something that she'll really like. It means you'll have to work extra hard at your spelling, though. Will you do that?"

"Oh yes," said Buttercup. "I noticed Fairy Gropplethorpe needs a new red scarf. I could try to magic up that."

"And her best woolly hat blew away in the wind," said Tingle. "I could try to magic up another one."

"Huh, that's nothing," said Scary Fairy. "I am going to magic up a new cloak AND new boots for her."

"Oh…" the other fairies fell silent. It was really hard to do that.

Airy Fairy looked sadly at her wand. It was a bit wonky since she'd poked Scary Fairy with it. What could she magic up for Fairy Gropplethorpe's Rainbow Birthday? What could she magic up that Fairy Gropplethorpe would like?

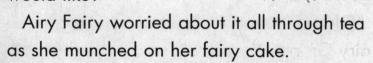

Airy Fairy worried about it all through tea as she munched on her fairy cake.

"Fairy Gropplethorpe was right," she said to Buttercup and Tingle. "There is so much to do in the springtime. First we have to spring clean our bedrooms for Miss Stickler's inspection, and I've only got one magic cleaning-up spell left. Then I have to paint my bedroom with only three magic spells. That's

really hard – I'll never win the fairy pen.
Finally I have to think up something special
for Fairy Gropplethorpe's Rainbow Birthday.
I'll never manage to do it all. I'm sure to get it
wrong."

"Stop worrying about it, Airy Fairy," said
Buttercup and Tingle. "You'll be fine."

"Oh no, you won't," muttered Scary Fairy,
listening in. "You'll be hopeless as usual. I'll
make sure of that."

Chapter Three

Later that evening, after the fairies had done their homework, they all went off to tidy their bedrooms.

"I've got to tidy mine up first time," Airy Fairy said to herself. "That's going to be tricky."

She looked around her room. It was a nice room. She had her little bed, a chair, a chest of drawers, and a big cupboard where she kept her school clothes. Sometimes. Most of the time they were over the chair, on the floor, or under the bed.

"It is a bit of a mess, I suppose," Airy Fairy muttered. "I wonder how those school socks got up on to the lightshade, and I don't remember leaving that banana skin on the floor. I'd better do as Miss Stickler says and use the tidy-up spell. Now how does it go?"

Airy Fairy thought and thought.

Is it,

Tidy up and
do it quick.

From the floor
my clothes all pick.

Or is it,
Spick and span,
span and spick.
Messy bedrooms
make me sick.

Or is it,
Everything is
in a heap.

Clean up all
I want to keep.

"Oh, I don't know," muttered Airy Fairy, and was just having a worry nibble at a fingernail when her bedroom door opened and Macduff wandered in.

Airy Fairy brightened up immediately. "Hullo, Macduff," she smiled, giving him a hug. "It's lovely to see you. You can help me tidy up, if you like."

Macduff wagged his tail and snuffled around. Airy Fairy's room was always full of good smells. He headed for Airy Fairy's bed, dived underneath, and came out crunching an old boiled sweet.

"Oh, well done, Macduff," said Airy Fairy. "I wondered where that had gone. I wonder what else is under there?" And she dived under the bed too.

"Oh look, Macduff, here's the box of chocolates Fairy Gropplethorpe gave me at Christmas time, and there are still some chocolates left. I'll share them with you so long as I can have all the coloured wrappers. I like to save them."

Macduff wagged his tail and Airy Fairy undid the foil wrappers, smoothed them out and put them into the pocket of her pink fairy frock. Then she shared out the chocolates. They were just on the last strawberry cream when they heard a voice outside in the corridor…

"Your bedroom is not too bad, Tingle, but go along to Scary Fairy's room and see what spotless really means."

"Oh no," gasped Airy Fairy, scrambling out from under the bed. "That's Miss Stickler and I haven't done any tidying at all. Now what's the right spell... I've only got one..." And she closed her eyes, waved her magic wand and said,

"*Spick and span,*
span and spick
Pick up everything
really quick,"
just as
Miss Stickler
came through
the door.

Immediately everything except Airy Fairy shot up into the air. Up went Macduff, the bed, the chair, the chest of drawers, the clothes that were lying about, and, worst of all, MISS STICKLER!

"Oh no," gasped Airy Fairy, as everything floated around her. "Oh no," she gasped again as her socks dropped on to Macduff's paws, and her spare knickers landed on Miss Stickler's head.

"Sorry, Miss Stickler," Airy Fairy gasped. "I'll just try another spell to make everything right…"

"Do NOT say another word, Airy Fairy,"
warned Miss Stickler, and waved her wand
to put things back in place. Everything
bumped down to the floor, including Miss
Stickler who landed on the banana skin,
skidded across the room, and hit her head
on the big cupboard.

She wasn't pleased. "You are a disgrace,
Airy Fairy," she stormed. "A disgrace to
yourself and a disgrace to this school.
When Fairy Gropplethorpe gets back, she
will hear all about it. In the meantime, you
will stay in every break-time till this room is
tidied up and completely spotless. And you
will do it WITHOUT the help of any spells.

If it's not done properly, you will not be allowed to paint your bedroom and you will lose your chance to win the special pen. Nor will you be allowed to magic up anything for Fairy Gropplethorpe's Rainbow Birthday. Do I make myself clear?"

"Yes, Miss Stickler. I'm very sorry, Miss Stickler," said Airy Fairy, and hung her head as Miss Stickler left.

To make matters worse, Scary Fairy poked her head round the door.

"What a mess," she said gleefully. "No wonder Aunt Stickler was annoyed. You'll never get to paint your bedroom now, Airy Fairy, and you'll be the only one without a present for Fairy Gropplethorpe. She won't think you're such a nice little fairy then, will she? Serves you right. I don't know why everyone likes you better than me anyway, you're such an idiot."

And Scary Fairy ran off laughing.

The other fairies heard Scary Fairy laughing and came to see what had happened.

"Oh dear," they said, when they heard.

"But don't worry, Airy Fairy," said Tingle.
"I'll wash the windows for you."

"And I'll sweep the floor," said Buttercup.

"We'll all help," promised the other fairies.

Late that night, while Miss Stickler and
Scary Fairy were fast asleep, the fairies flew
around the silent school and gathered
together buckets and mops.

Then they slipped into Airy Fairy's room and
helped her spring clean. Even Macduff
helped by eating up all the cake crumbs.

Airy Fairy couldn't believe it. Her bedroom had never been so tidy.

"It's not just tidy," she gasped. "It's spotless. Thank you all so much."

"That's what friends are for," smiled the other fairies, and went off to get some sleep.

But Airy Fairy couldn't sleep. She couldn't wait to show Miss Stickler her spotless bedroom. Immediately after breakfast next morning, she asked Miss Stickler to come and inspect it.

When she saw it, Miss Stickler gasped, "I don't believe it. This bedroom is almost as clean as Scary Fairy's. How did you manage it?"

"I was up all night," said Airy Fairy truthfully.

"Well, I don't know how you've done it, Airy Fairy, but your bedroom is spotless. You may now use the three spells to paint it."

"Thank you, Miss Stickler."

All the fairies were delighted for Airy Fairy, except Scary Fairy.

"How did you do it?" she scowled during morning lessons. "I bet you cheated and did some extra spells."

"No, I didn't," said Airy Fairy. "I'm hopeless at spelling. You said so yourself."

Scary Fairy scowled even harder. "You're up to something," she said. "But you'd better look out. I've got my eye on you."

But Airy Fairy didn't hear. She had closed her eyes, put her head down on her fairy notebook and was fast asleep.

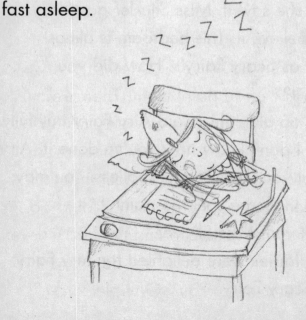

Chapter Four

That afternoon Miss Stickler was in a good mood.

"Now that all your rooms are tidy and spotless," she said, "I've decided to give you the afternoon off to paint them. Then we must get on with magicking up our presents for Fairy Gropplethorpe's Rainbow Birthday. I hope you've been thinking about that too."

"I've been thinking there's such a lot to do," said Airy Fairy to Buttercup and Tingle. "I'll never get it all done in time, and I still don't know what to magic up for Fairy Gropplethorpe."

"Whatever it is, it'll be something stupid," said Scary Fairy. "I'm already working on my presents. The cloak and boots are going to be beautiful. Fairy Gropplethorpe's sure to like them best."

"Do stop talking, Fairies," said Miss Stickler, "and go and paint your bedrooms. Be sure to change your clothes first – and TRY not to make TOO much mess, Airy Fairy."

Airy Fairy went upstairs to her bedroom and found Macduff fast asleep on her bed.

"Poor old Macduff," she said, stroking his floppy ears. "Like me, you really do miss Fairy Gropplethorpe, don't you?"

Macduff snuffled and licked her hand.

"But you can help me decide what colour to paint my bedroom, if you like."

But Macduff just wrinkled his nose and went back to sleep.

Airy Fairy smiled. "I'll go and see what Buttercup's doing. Perhaps she'll give me an idea."

Airy Fairy tripped along the corridor to Buttercup's room and tapped on the door.

"Come in," called Buttercup.

"Ooh, Buttercup," said Airy Fairy. "Your room's lovely. It's like walking into sunshine."

"Thank you," grinned Buttercup. "I'm so glad you like it. It took all three spells to get the colour just right. What colour are you going to choose?"

"Not sure yet," said Airy Fairy. "I'm going to look at Tingle's room."

Tingle's door was wide open and Airy Fairy gasped when she saw the colour of her bedroom walls.

"Wow, Tingle!" she said. "Your room's amazing. Like a fantastic sunset."

"Thank you," said Tingle. "I'm really pleased with it, but it took all three spells to get the colour just right. What colour are you going to choose?"

"Not sure yet," sighed Airy Fairy, and wandered back along the corridor past Scary Fairy's room. Her door was open too, and her room was painted eye-watering electric pink.

Like an explosion in Mr Goblin's gobstopper factory, thought Airy Fairy.

When Scary Fairy caught sight of her, she flew out and grabbed her arm. "Have you painted your room yet?" she demanded.

"No," said Airy Fairy. "I'm not sure what colour to make it."

"Well, don't go copying mine. Pink is THE fairy colour and since I'm the best fairy, I get to choose it."

"I'll choose whatever colour I like," said Airy Fairy. "But don't worry, it won't be sickly pickly pink like yours."

"My room is NOT sickly pickly pink," said Scary Fairy and stamped her foot. "I'll turn your hair itchy twitchy witchy for that," and she raised her little wand. But Airy Fairy was too quick for her and she flipped the wand out of Scary Fairy's hand. It sailed over the bannister, twirled down to the big hall below, and rolled underneath a large table.

"How dare you!" Scary Fairy yelled. "Fetch my wand back this minute!"

"Oh, go and kiss a warty toad." Airy Fairy grinned and wandered on.

Scary Fairy made a really scary face. "I'll get you for that, Airy Fairy," she muttered. "Just see if I don't."

But Airy Fairy was too busy worrying about colours to notice.

When she got back to her room, Macduff opened one eye and yawned.

"I think I've decided on a colour," she told him. "I'm going to paint my room the colour of the sea." And she closed her eyes and said the spell,

"Turquoise blue and softest green.
Make my room a seaside dream."

ZIP! Two paint pots and two paint brushes appeared and sailed through the air towards Airy Fairy, spilling turquoise blue and softest green paint all over the floor.

"Hey, watch what you're doing!" yelled

Airy Fairy. But they didn't. They splashed blue and green paint all over the walls and all over the furniture.

Then, ZIP! The two paint pots and brushes disappeared as quickly as they'd come.

"What a mess!" cried Airy Fairy. She was so upset, she didn't hear Scary Fairy giggling outside her door.

"Oh Macduff," wailed Airy Fairy. "Just look at my room. Fairy Gropplethorpe won't be pleased and Miss Stickler will be furious. I'll have to use another spell to sort it out."

Macduff closed both eyes as Airy Fairy closed hers and said the spell,

"Clean and wipe and wipe and clean.
Make my room fit to be seen."

ZIP! Two washcloths and two buckets appeared and sailed through the air towards Airy Fairy. The wet cloths flapped about the room soaking the walls, the furniture and the floor. Soon everywhere was dripping wet.

Then, ZIP! The washcloths and the buckets left as quickly as they had come.

"Come back!" yelled Airy Fairy. "You haven't finished yet. Now my room looks worse than ever." But they didn't come back, and Airy Fairy was so upset, she didn't hear Scary Fairy giggling fit to burst outside her door.

Airy Fairy was in despair. "My room looks terrible and I only have one spell left. Oh, I wish I was better at spelling. I've got to get it right this time."

Macduff, splashed with water and paint, sat with his paws over his eyes as Airy Fairy closed her eyes and said the spell,

"Magic darkness, magic light.

Help me make my room all right."

ZIP! A large cloud appeared and enveloped Airy Fairy.

"Help help," she cried. "Where did everything go? What's happening? I can't see a thing."

Then ZIP! The cloud disappeared as quickly as it had come, and Airy Fairy looked around.

"Oh no," she cried. "I asked you to make my room all right, not all white. Now the walls are back to the colour they were to begin with."

And this time she did hear a loud laugh outside her bedroom door and just glimpsed the tip of a little wand. She opened the door wider and was just in time to see Scary Fairy disappear down the corridor. She was still laughing.

"Oh no," cried Airy Fairy. "I should have known it was Scary Fairy up to her rotten tricks. She's always getting me into trouble. Miss Stickler and Fairy Gropplethorpe will think I've been really lazy and haven't tried to paint my room at all! I can't let them think that. I must do something. But what?"

Chapter Five

For the rest of that day, Airy Fairy sat in her room and thought and thought. *How can I paint these walls in time for Fairy Gropplethorpe coming back?*

She asked the other fairies who popped in to see her. They thought and thought too.

"Sorry, Airy Fairy," they all said finally. "We've used up all our spells, so we don't know either."

Airy Fairy sighed and cuddled Macduff. He wagged his tail and knocked over her alarm clock.

Airy Fairy picked it up. "Oops, look at the time, Macduff. Time to go to the kitchen to get your supper."

Macduff wagged his tail again and followed Airy Fairy down to the kitchen. Airy Fairy went to the big store cupboard where Fairy Gropplethorpe kept his food, and looked inside. There were rows and rows of tinned dog food. Macduff shuffled forward and snuffled at a tin on the bottom row.

"Do you want that one?" asked Airy Fairy. Macduff wagged his tail and Airy Fairy pulled out the tin. All the other tins of dog food collasped in a heap round about her.

"Oh no," she wailed. "Everything is in a mess today."

But then she saw some other tins piled up behind the dog food.

"Paint tins," breathed Airy Fairy. "With different colours of paint. I could choose one of those, and paint my room myself. Fairy Gropplethorpe wouldn't mind." And she lifted out a sky blue one and looked inside. "I like the colour," she said,"but there's not enough paint left to paint my room. I'll try the soft lilac one. I like that colour too." And she lifted it down and looked inside. "Oh no, there's not enough paint left in that one either."

She tried all the other paint tins, but they were all the same. None of them had enough paint left to paint a fairy bedroom.

While Macduff munched his supper Airy Fairy sat down among the paint tins to have a think. She looked at the names on the tins. Sky Blue. Soft Lilac. Sunshine Yellow. Spring Green. SPRING GREEN! Airy Fairy jumped up.

"That's it, Macduff," she cried. "I've got it. I'll use all the colours in the paint pots to paint my bedroom."

Later that night, when everyone else was fast asleep, Macduff watched as Airy Fairy flew up and down the stairs carrying as many paint pots as she could.

"That should do it," she puffed, as she looked at all the tins in the middle of her bedroom floor. "Now what should I begin with?" Then she remembered how nice the school had looked in the spring sunshine. She remembered the bowls of spring flowers in the hall, and she remembered the fat buds on the oak tree. And she smiled, dipped her paintbrush into the first pot and began to paint.

Dawn was lightening the sky by the time she had finished and ferried all the paint pots back to the store, and it was a very sleepy Airy Fairy who sat down at her desk for morning lessons.

Scary Fairy poked her awake with her wand. "Have you decided on a colour to paint your bedroom yet?" she giggled.

"Why are you asking?" said Airy Fairy. "You know very well you magicked up a mess."

"But you can't prove it," smirked Scary Fairy. "And I bet Fairy Gropplethorpe will be really cross with you for not even TRYING to win the special pen." And she sat back, looking very pleased with herself.

Two minutes later Miss Stickler came bustling into the classroom. "Fairies, Fairies," she cried. "A terrible thing has happened. It seems I have made a mistake."

The fairies all looked at each other. Miss Stickler make a mistake? That had never happened before.

"I have got the date of Fairy Gropplethorpe's Rainbow Birthday wrong. I thought it was tomorrow, but it's not, it's today. Fairy Gropplethorpe will be back from her conference shortly, and I must organize her birthday tea. This morning, therefore, you must finish off your special presents for her. I hope you're all making something really nice." And she hurried off to the kitchen to make a birthday cake.

"I'm glad my scarf for Fairy Gropplethorpe's nearly finished," said Buttercup. "I just have to work out the spell for putting some fringes on the ends."

"My woolly hat's nearly finished too," said Tingle. "I just have to work out the spell for putting a bobble on the top."

"My cloak and boots have been finished for ages," boasted Scary Fairy. "But then I am the best at spelling, as well as everything else."

And she turned to Airy Fairy and said. "What have you made for Fairy Gropplethorpe's Rainbow Birthday? I bet it's something stupid."

"No, it's not," said Airy Fairy, "because I've had so much to do, I haven't made anything yet."

"Then you'll be the only one without anything for Fairy Gropplethorpe. You really are in trouble, Airy Fairy. Serves you right. You're such an idiot!" And Scary Fairy flew away laughing.

Chapter Six

Airy Fairy sat and listened to what all the
other fairies were making for Fairy
Gropplethorpe's Rainbow Birthday. Cherri
was making her a new shopping basket.
Twin fairies Twink and Plink were making her
new gloves, one each. Honeysuckle had
designed a fantastic frilly parasol. "For the
sunny days ahead," she smiled. And Silvie
and Skelf were working on a matching
necklace and bracelet.

"What does that leave for me to make?"
wondered Airy Fairy. And she sat in the
classroom, with her elbows on her desk and her
chin in her hands, after the others had gone.

She looked out of the window. The oak buds
had just burst and tiny green leaves were
stretching themselves out towards the sunshine.

"I knew they would do that when I wasn't
looking," she said.

And she was so busy looking at the new
leaves, she didn't notice Scary Fairy keeping
an eye on her through the classroom door.

But she did notice the red squirrel leaping
around among the branches of the oak tree.

"Hullo, Mr Squirrel," she called. "I'd love to come out and play with you, but I've got to magic up a present for Fairy Gropplethorpe's Rainbow Birthday, and I don't know what to make." Then she noticed the red squirrel nibbling away on a nut and that gave her an idea.

"I know what I can do," she cried. "I can magic up some chocolates for Fairy Gropplethorpe. She likes chocolates." And Airy Fairy closed her eyes and said the spell,

"Creamy-centred luscious chocs.
Send them down
in a pretty box."

THUNK! A large brown box dropped on to the floor.

"Oh dear," said Airy Fairy. "That doesn't look like what I asked for."

She peeped inside. It wasn't a box of chocs. It was a box of rocks. Big ones, small ones, jaggy ones, craggy ones.

"Now how did that happen?" said Airy Fairy. "I was sure I had got the spell right. Perhaps I had better look up Miss Stickler's Big Book of Spells to check."

Outside the classroom door, Scary Fairy giggled. "That won't do you any good. Not while I'm around."

Airy Fairy was just looking through the Big Book of Spells when she had another idea.

"Fairy Gropplethorpe loves books. I could magic up a Big Book of Fairy Tales for her Rainbow Birthday."

And she closed her eyes and said the
spell,

"*Stories of giants, mermaids and whales.*
I'd like a Big Book of Fairy Tales."

WHUMP! A whole pile of hairy tails fell
down. There were curly ones, straight ones,
stripy ones and spiky ones.

"Oi, get off me!" yelled Airy Fairy. "I'm
sure I didn't ask for hairy tails."

Outside the classroom door, Scary Fairy was laughing fit to burst. She was having a great time upsetting Airy Fairy's spells.

But Airy Fairy wasn't giving up.

"Well, magicking up a box of chocs and a book haven't got me anywhere," she muttered. "What else would Fairy Gropplethorpe like?"

She thought and thought. *She's already getting a cloak and boots, a hat and scarf, a parasol and gloves, a necklace and bracelet, and a basket. What else is there?*

"I know," she cried. "Perfume. Fairy Gropplethorpe likes to dab a little behind her ears. I'll do the spell for that."

And she closed her eyes and said the spell,
"Roses, pansies, scented flocks.
Send some perfume in a box."
EUGH! It started raining smelly socks.

"Oh no," wailed Airy Fairy. "I'm sure I didn't ask for smelly socks."

Outside the classroom door, Scary Fairy was holding her sides. Then she saw Miss Stickler coming round the corner and she flew away, sharpish. Miss Stickler hurried along to the classroom.

"Help," she cried, as she tripped over the box of rocks and landed in among the pile of hairy tails and smelly socks.

"Airy Fairy!" she yelled. "I might have guessed. If there's a mess, you're bound to be responsible for it."

"But I was only trying to magic up a present for Fairy Gropplethorpe's Rainbow Birthday," protested Airy Fairy.

"Too late for that now," said Miss Stickler. "Fairy Gropplethorpe has arrived. Now hurry along to the hall and take your place with the other fairies for the Rainbow Birthday surprise."

Airy Fairy went along to the hall. All the other fairies were there with their presents. The presents looked beautiful, especially Scary Fairy's cloak and boots.

"See what I magicked up for Fairy Gropplethorpe," she said. "A bit better than a box of rocks or hairy tails or smelly socks, isn't it, Airy Fairy?"

Airy Fairy sighed. She should have watched out for Scary Fairy.

Then Fairy Gropplethorpe came into the hall, followed by Macduff, nearly wagging his tail off. He was so pleased to see her.

"Happy Rainbow Birthday!" all the fairies cried, and to Fairy Gropplethorpe's surprise and delight, they presented her with their gifts.

Airy Fairy hung back. She had nothing to give Fairy Gropplethorpe for her special birthday. Then she looked at Macduff and remembered sitting on the floor of her bedroom with him, eating the last of the Christmas chocolates. Then she remembered putting the coloured foil wrappers in her pocket.

Then she had an idea. She took the
wrappers out and secretly made them into
a neat little shape. That done, she smiled,
closed her eyes and whispered the spell,

"Not a glove, not a hat,
not a bright woolly mitten.

Please send me down
a small rainbow kitten."

MIAOW. At her feet appeared the tiniest,
stripiest kitten Airy Fairy had ever seen.
Airy Fairy grinned, picked
her up, and took her to
Fairy Gropplethorpe.

"Happy Rainbow Birthday, Fairy Gropplethorpe!" she said. "I hope you like the rainbow kitten. I hope Macduff likes her too. He was a little bit lonely while you were away."

"Oh, thank you, Airy Fairy," beamed Fairy Gropplethorpe. "How thoughtful of you. I just love her. I'll call her Rainbow, of course. What do you think, Macduff?"

Macduff gave a big happy WUFF! and wagged his tail in circles.

Scary Fairy scowled. How had Airy Fairy managed it? It was easy to see Fairy Gropplethorpe really liked the kitten.

"Let's have the birthday tea now," said Miss Stickler. "I've made you a special cake, Fairy Gropplethorpe."

"Oh, can't we show Fairy Gropplethorpe our newly painted bedrooms first, Aunt Stickler?" said Scary Fairy. She was sure THAT would get Airy Fairy into trouble and she was sure SHE would win the special pen.

"Of course," said Miss Stickler. "I'd nearly forgotten." And she led the way upstairs.

Fairy Gropplethorpe was delighted at how neat and clean and bright the newly painted bedrooms were.

"You've had so much to do and you've worked very hard," she said to the fairies. "Well done."

"Just wait till she gets to your room," Scary Fairy smirked to Airy Fairy.

Airy Fairy's bedroom was last, and when Miss Stickler opened the door, everyone gasped. Inside it was springtime. On one white wall, Airy Fairy had painted a large oak tree, and nestling in its branches was Fairy Gropplethorpe's Academy for Good Fairies. Spring sunshine shone on the school, making its windows sparkle. On the branches, green leaves were just opening up, and ten tiny fairies and a red squirrel played among them. On a sturdy branch sat Miss Stickler, Fairy Gropplethorpe and Macduff, while underneath, a spring garden bloomed. The garden wound its way round the other walls where Airy Fairy had painted little animals and birds playing in the spring sunshine.

Fairy Gropplethorpe clapped her hands. "Oh, how splendid, Airy Fairy," she said. "What a wonderful idea."

"I had to use the spare paint from the tins in the cupboard downstairs because my spells didn't work out very well," said Airy Fairy truthfully.

"Then you've worked really hard indeed," smiled Fairy Gropplethorpe. "I don't think there's any doubt that this is the best bedroom, and that Airy Fairy deserves the prize. Don't you agree, Miss Stickler?"

Miss Stickler opened her mouth to protest, then just nodded. Scary Fairy made a face that was really scary.

"But I'm afraid, before you get the special pen, Airy Fairy, you'll have to get the paint tins out again because there's something you've forgotten to put in the picture."

Airy Fairy looked all round the walls. She screwed up her eyes and looked all round again.

"I don't know…"

Buttercup and Tingle smiled at each other and nudged Airy Fairy. "Miaow," they giggled.

"Oh, I know what it is now." Airy Fairy grinned. "I've still to paint in a rainbow kitten."

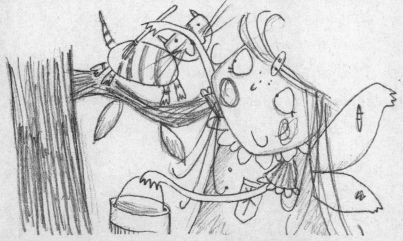

Meet Airy Fairy.
Her wand is all wonky, her wings
are covered in sticking plaster
and her spells are always a muddle!
But she's the cutest fairy around!

Look out for the other
books in this series.

Margaret Ryan

Airy Fairy

Magic Mischief!

How can one little
fairy get into such
BIG trouble?

■■ SCHOLASTIC

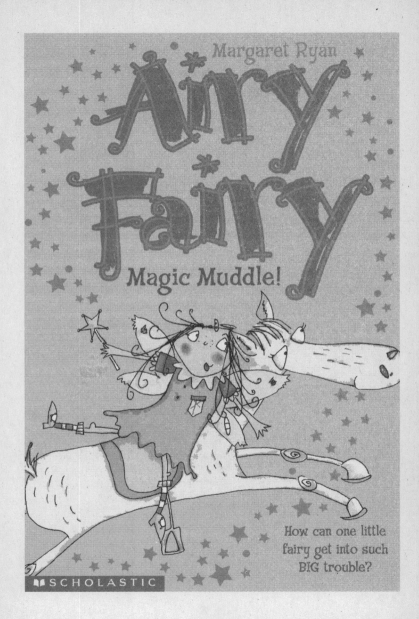

Margaret Ryan

Airy Fairy

Magic Muddle!

How can one little
fairy get into such
BIG trouble?

SCHOLASTIC